Shoe Town

Shoe Town

Written by Janet Stevens and
Susan Stevens Crummel
Illustrated by Janet Stevens

Green Light Readers
Harcourt, Inc.
Orlando   Austin   New York   San Diego   London

There was a little mouse
who had a little shoe.

When her babies grew up,
she knew just what to do.

"I'll fill a hot bath,
then I'll take a long nap."

Just then at her shoe
came a *rap-tap-tap-tap*.

"We are Tortoise and Hare.
We just went for a run.

Can we stay here with you . . .
in your shoe? Oh, what fun!"

"My shoe is too little
for so many to share.

Look for a shoe, if you please.
It can go over there."

"Now I'll fill a hot bath,
then I'll take a long nap."

Just then at her shoe
came a *rap-tap-tap-tap*.

"I'm the Little Red Hen.
And I love making bread.

Is there room in your shoe
for one more?" she said.

"My shoe is too little
for so many to share.

"Hey-diddle-diddle-door, Now there are four!"

Look for a shoe, if you please.
It can go over there."

"Now I'll fill a hot bath,
then I'll take a long nap."

Just then at her shoe
came a big *RAP-TAP-TAP!*

"I'll huff and I'll puff
and I'll blow your shoes down—

if you don't let me stay
in your little shoe town!"

"Don't huff and don't puff.
We'll be happy to share.

Look for a shoe, if you please.
It can go over there."

More and more friends came.
The little town grew.

And to think it began
with a mouse and her shoe!

My Shoe Town

Make shoe houses for your favorite storybook characters.

- paper
- pencil
- crayons or markers
- scissors
- stapler

1 Put your shoes on.

2 Stand on a piece of paper.

3 Trace your shoes with a pencil.

4 Cut out the paper shoes and staple them together.

5 On one side, draw the outside of the storybook character's house.

6 On the other side, draw the character inside the house.

7 Make more houses so you have a whole shoe town.

8 Tell stories about your shoes and the characters who live in them!

Meet the Coauthors and Illustrator

Susan Stevens Crummel   *Janet Stevens*

   Janet Stevens and Susan Stevens Crummel are sisters who grew up all over the United States. Janet has loved art ever since she can remember. She is often asked how she learned to draw so well. Her answer is: "Lots and lots of practice!" Susan likes to write as often as she can. She especially loves writing stories with her sister.

   Janet and Susan wrote *Shoe Town* together. First, Janet had a good story idea. Then Susan put it into words. Both Janet and Susan feel that this teamwork was very exciting. They had a lot of fun putting characters from other stories, like the Little Red Hen, in *Shoe Town*!

For information about permission to reproduce selections from this book,
write to trade.permissions@hmhco.com or to Permissions, Houghton Mifflin Harcourt
Publishing Company, 3 Park Avenue, 19th Floor, New York, New York 10016.

www.hmhco.com

First Green Light Readers edition 1999
Green Light Readers is a trademark of Harcourt, Inc., registered in the
United States of America and/or other jurisdictions.

The Library of Congress has cataloged an earlier edition as follows:
Stevens, Janet.
Shoe town/written by Janet Stevens and Susan Stevens Crummel;
illustrated by Janet Stevens.
p. cm.
"Green Light Readers."
Summary: As she tries to settle down for a nap, a mouse who lives in a shoe is visited
first by Tortoise and Hare, then by Little Red Hen, and lastly by the Big Bad Wolf.
[1. Mice—Fiction. 2. Characters in literature—Fiction. 3. Shoes—Fiction.
4. Stories in rhyme.] I. Crummel, Susan Stevens. II. Title.
PZ8.3.S844Sh 1999
[E]—dc21 98-15564
ISBN 978-0-15-204882-2
ISBN 978-0-15-204842-6 (pb)

SCP 15 14 13 12
4500644012

Ages 5–7
Grades: 1–2
Guided Reading Level: G–I
Reading Recovery Level: 15–16

Green Light Readers
For the reader who's ready to GO!

"A must-have for any family with a beginning reader."—*Boston Sunday Herald*

"You can't go wrong with adding several copies of these terrific books to your beginning-to-read collection."—*School Library Journal*

"A winner for the beginner."—*Booklist*

Five Tips to Help Your Child Become a Great Reader

1. Get involved. Reading aloud to and with your child is just as important as encouraging your child to read independently.

2. Be curious. Ask questions about what your child is reading.

3. Make reading fun. Allow your child to pick books on subjects that interest her or him.

4. Words are everywhere—not just in books. Practice reading signs, packages, and cereal boxes with your child.

5. Set a good example. Make sure your child sees YOU reading.

Why Green Light Readers Is the Best Series for Your New Reader

● Created exclusively for beginning readers by some of the biggest and brightest names in children's books

● Reinforces the reading skills your child is learning in school

● Encourages children to read—and finish—books by themselves

● Offers extra enrichment through fun, age-appropriate activities unique to each story

● Incorporates characteristics of the Reading Recovery program used by educators

● Developed with Harcourt School Publishers and credentialed educational consultants